Point Man in
Your Pocket

A Forty–Day March with Jesus

Chuck Dean

173rd Abn. Bde, Vietnam 1965-66

POINT MAN IN YOUR POCKET
Copyright © 1997 by Chuck Dean

Published by WordSmith Publishing

Except where noted, all Scripture verses are from the New
American Standard version of the Bible. Copyright © 1976,
1978 by the Moody Bible Institute of Chicago.

1 Corinthians 1:8-10 used from *The Living Bible*,
Copyright © 1971 Tyndale House Publishers.

ISBN 1-57921-027-9
Library of Congress Number: 97-60775

"I think you ought to know, dear brothers, about the hard time we went through in Asia. We were really crushed and overwhelmed, and feared we would never live through it. We felt we were doomed to die and saw how powerless we were to help ourselves; but that was good, for then we put everything into the hands of God, who alone could save us, for He can even raise the dead. And He did help us, and saved us from a terrible death; yes, and we expect him to do it again and again."

2 Corinthians 1:8–10 (TLB)

CONTENTS

Onward..6
Day 1   The Full Armor of God................................8
Day 2   The Army in Which I Choose to Fight...........10
Day 3   No Lone Patrols...12
Day 4   Moving Over, Through or Around Obstacles..13
Day 5   Cutting the Pie..15
Day 6   But If Not...16
Day 7   Combat Readiness......................................20
Day 8   Offensive War..22
Day 9   Jesus is Victor..24
Day 10   Dream Sheet...25
Day 11   The Suffering of Soldiers............................27
Day 12   Doors...29
Day 13   Don't Forget Your Buddy.............................31
Day 14   Line of March...32
Day 15   Patriotism...33
Day 16   Tattoos..34
Day 17   Following Orders.......................................36
Day 18   The Same God...37

Day 19 The Mission.................................38

Day 20 Sacrifice.....................................40

Day 21 Reform the Lines and Attack!.......................42

Day 22 Volunteers and Draftees.......................44

Day 23 Light on the Path.......................46

Day 24 Let the Past Be the Past at Last.................47

Day 25 Surrendering.......................49

Day 26 Fear...50

Day 27 Hardship.......................51

Day 28 Wounds.......................52

Day 29 Survival Skills.......................53

Day 30 God Loves Failures.......................54

Day 31 Choosing Sides.......................55

Day 32 Laying Tracks.......................56

Day 33 The Elite Soldier.......................58

Day 34 Rearguard.......................60

Day 35 Reveille.......................61

Day 36 The Night is Over.......................62

Day 37 Follow Me.......................63

Day 38 Taking Prisoners.......................64

Day 39 A Soldier's Confession.......................65

Day 40 The Long March.......................66

Onward

A point man is the soldier who walks out in front of a combat unit on the march. He is the eyes and ears for his trailing companions. The point man "points" the way in which to go, watching for enemy traps and ambushes to make sure the unit makes it safely through dangerous terrain.

Soldiers do best when they are led by example. A unit's discipline and effectiveness will reflect how its leader has set the example for their conduct. When Jesus came to live with us, it was the first and only time that God came to earth. He appeared to set an example—a pattern for us to march by.

1 John 3:8 gives a simple explanation of why God chose to come to earth, *"The Son of God appeared for this purpose, that He might destroy the works of the devil."* And then in Hebrews 2:14–18 we also see that God took on human form and *"had to be made like His brothers…"* so that He could lead His army by example.

The most classic forty–day period of time in all of human history took place when the Spirit of God led Jesus into the wilderness to begin His warfare against the devil mentioned in 1 John 3:8, *"And immediately the Spirit impelled Him to go out into the wilderness. And He was in the wilderness forty days being tempted by Satan; and He was with the wild beasts, and the angels were ministering to Him."* He was prepared in those forty days to stand against the devices of the enemy, and this is our example.

Point Man in Your Pocket is a forty–day march for those who want more of God in their life. There is no better point man than Jesus, so I encourage you to put on your gear and take the journey. Pray along the way—fast if that suits your fancy—and let it be your companion as you march through the war zones of life.

Day 1

The Full Armor of God

*Put on the full armor of God that
you may be able to stand firm
against the schemes of the devil.*
Ephesians 6:11

It's a good practice to put on God's full armor as we begin each day. Many Christians don't take the time or make the effort to *pray their armor on* before starting the daily march. This is asking for trouble and when we don't have it on, the enemy is the first to notice.

In a war zone, we never go on patrol without all the necessary equipment to survive combat. Being in God's army is no different, and He expects us to take up *His* armor to repel the assaults of the enemy.

I encourage you to study Ephesians 6:10–18 and Isaiah 58:8. And next, make it a point—a daily discipline to put on the full armor of God in prayer. Here is an example of how to do that:

"I put on the belt of truth, that today I speak and hear only the truth of God.

"I put on the breastplate of righteousness, that my heart is protected by God. That I would have a right standing before God and His throne today.

"I shod my feet with the gospel of peace, that everywhere I step God's peace will abound.

"I take up the shield of faith to ward off the fiery darts of the enemy. Jesus, I proclaim You to be my shield; a shield that I can kneel down behind and seek protection from the enemy.

"I put on the helmet of salvation, that my mind will be protected by God. Lord, transform my mind into the mind of Christ this day, that all the thoughts that I have will be the thoughts of Jesus Himself.

"I take up the Sword of the Spirit—the Word of God— to wield against the enemy. I also pray that this Sword may be used to circumcise my own fleshly heart. Let the Word of God give me strength this day to rise above the sin that abounds in my life and in this world.

"Lord I thank you for protecting my backside with Your Glory as proclaimed in Isaiah 58:8. The Lord God almighty is my rearguard, and I do not have to be afraid of what is behind me. Amen."

Day 2

The Army in Which I Choose to Fight

For day by day men came to David to help him,
until there was a great army like the army of God.
1 Chronicles 12:22

God's people have two armies. One is set up for display with lovely guns and neat little soldiers—all in a row. It has socially-correct staffs schooled in etiquette and distinguished generals swaggering through the ranks as if they were the Almighty Himself. It's core is made up of sunshine soldiers and fair-weather patriots who leave the dirty work to others. Here's an army that shows itself, for a modest fee, on any Sunday morning parade field— steeped in traditional salutes, precision drills and a week-end-warrior mentality.

The other is a real army composed entirely of enthusiastic Christian soldiers in battle attire—who will not be put on display, but from whom impossible efforts are demanded. Their standard is the Word of God. The Sword of Truth is their primary weapon. This is the army in which I choose to fight.

Occasionally, I meet other soldiers who have made this choice. When I do, it's like an old soldier's dream: where the team is a team, and everyone respects the other's spiritual gifts and God-given authority. The generals, colonels, lieutenants and sergeants lead by humble example, and all follow the tough commandments of God's written Word. There is no compromise. This is the army in which I choose to fight.

Day 3

No Lone Patrols

...Then Jesus sent two disciples...
Matthew 21:1

Patrols and combat missions are never done alone. We are sent out in twos or more. Look for a friend to enlist with, and walk with them through the problems that arise today.

It is easy, but foolish, to think that we are tough enough to hack it all by ourselves. God wants us to fight the battles as a unit, not as individuals—He knows there is strength in numbers, *"For where two or three come together in my name, there I am with them."* (Matthew 18:20)

Day 4

Moving Over, Through or Around Obstacles

Consider it all joy, my brother,
when you encounter various trials,
knowing that the testing of your
faith produces endurance.

James 1:2–3

Soldiers who hope to survive on a battlefield learn the art of negotiating over, through, and around obstacles that hinder their direction of travel. There may be bomb craters, fallen trees, rivers, jungles, mountains, rocks or barbwire configurations that can slow down the line of march. This is why every basic training area has an "obstacle course" to practice on.

The longer we serve as Christian soldiers the more aware we become of life's obstacles; we also begin to recognize traps and ambushes the enemy sets for us. If you have

13

not learned how to move across the battlefield correctly, you will have needless frustrations along the march. Your progress will be slow.

If you are blocked today and feel cut off in your walk with God, try submitting each obstacle you face, one at a time, to the Lord. He is there to lead you through, but remember this: You cannot carry all that you own onto this battlefield; your baggage will weigh you down. You must give it to Jesus to carry for you. *"Cast your burden upon the Lord, and he will sustain you..."* (Psalm 55:22a). He is your Point Man—let Him take the lead.

Day 5

Cutting the Pie

*For I have been informed concerning
you...that there are quarrels among you.*

1 Corinthians 1:11

There was a principle of warfare in Viet Nam that the Viet Cong used against us quite effectively. It was a tactical principle initiated in guerrilla warfare that we called "cutting the pie."

As evening approached we would stop our operations in the jungle and set up a night defense perimeter. We would dig in to protect ourselves until morning.

In this large circle of dug-in troops (better known as the "pie"), the most important equipment and the command post usually went in the center. It was our responsibility as riflemen to secure our section of the perimeter. We dug in by pairs and one slept while the other kept watch for enemy movement and intrusion. The enemy also viewed our perimeter as a large pie, and their objec-

15

tive was to slice it up into little pieces...hoping to overrun
the whole unit bit by bit.

They would make a probe (test the strength of our perimeter and create a disturbance along the line). Then
pull back into the jungle. By doing this they hoped that
we would fire blindly in the direction of the disturbance.
Of course, if we did fire at them we would hit our own
men on the perimeter to our left or right, because the real
enemy was no longer there. The VC would take a big slice
out of the "pie" by having us kill each other when we
thought we were shooting at them.

In the realm of relationships our "enemy" does the same
thing. He moves in and causes some commotion, and then
pulls back. Since we cannot see him, we begin to fire in
the direction of the noise—and hit our brothers or sisters
who are on the other side of the defense perimeter.

We shoot, wound, and even kill them, but the real enemy goes undetected. He is allowed to continue his ha-
rassment within the ranks.

We need to know who our real enemy is, (*"...be on the
alert, your adversary, **the devil**, prowls about like a roaring
lion, looking for someone to devour."* 1 Peter 5:8). Remember, in all your ups and downs...no man or woman is your
enemy...if someone is coming against you, they are only

being *used* to make noise...don't shoot until you've identified the real enemy—and then fire away in the Name of Jesus!

Day 6

But If Not

...our God whom we serve will deliver us
from the furnace of blazing fire; and He
will deliver us out of your hand, O king.
Daniel 3:17

During World War II Winston Churchill, and his staff, waited anxiously to hear some word from the beleaguered British Army at Dunkirk.

Across the Channel the troops faced overwhelming odds as the Nazi Army marched on their positions... there was seemingly no hope of stopping them. The Prime Minister, and all of England, had not heard a word from their men for the longest time. Then suddenly the wire came alive and as the country's leadership crowded around to hear the message from the front lines, they were put at ease when all that came over the wire from the combat units was, "But if not..."

What did this mean? How could these three little words give comfort? Churchill and the others who had been scholars of the Bible knew precisely what it meant. It meant that their army was willing to fight to the last man in spite of anything thrown at them—they had driven in their stake and committed their lives to the fight. The message was a reference to a portion of Scripture in the Book of Daniel. It was about three young men who also refused to give up—and would rather die than do so.

These young men—Shadrach, Meshach and Abednego—were told by a wicked, ungodly king to renounce God and he would spare their lives. He threatened to throw them into a burning furnace. In unison, they turned to the king and answered him, *"Go ahead and throw us in the fire because the God whom we serve will deliver us from this pain and death, and He will deliver us out of your hand also, O king. BUT IF NOT, let it be known that we will still not renounce Him or serve you and your gods."*

You can take a stand just like that today. You don't have to compromise your beliefs, and there is no need for fear. Your faith will see you through. Drive in your stake for Jesus; don't budge, He will deliver you.

Day 7

Combat Readiness

Whom shall I send, and who will go for Us?
Then I said, "Here am I. Send me!"
Isaiah 6:8

The soldier who is ready to serve God and do His work is the one decorated with honor after the call to arms is over. Readiness means having a right relationship with the "Supreme Commander" and knowing what He wants. Most of the time, however, we are so busy telling God what we want to do and where we want to go, that we miss His "orders of the day." We may be waiting for the perfect duty, or the sensational assignment—one that most likely will glorify us instead of God—to come along before we act. When that "glorious" and great opportunity does arrive, we are the first to step out of the ranks and say, "Here I am. Send me!" However, are we

20

ready to accept the dirty, obscure and undistinguished little duty assignment when He calls us to it?

Combat readiness means that we are ready to do the smallest thing or the largest—it makes no difference. Today, be mindful that God may place you in a wonderful and pleasant duty assignment, or He may lead you to a drab and thankless place. Will you be ready for both?

Day 8

Offensive War

*Press on toward the goal for the prize
of the upward call of God in Jesus Christ.*
Philippians 3:14

In warfare, the offensive is the means by which one takes an objective. It is an aggressive advance against an enemy to take from him what he possesses.

Offensive warfare give soldiers a moral and physical advantage when engaging in combat. The attacking military leaders have the advantage of making decisions first and then the thrust to carry them out.

On the other hand, a defending army must wait to see what the aggressor will do before they can make their own decision on how to fight.

Don't be on the defensive today. Press on to do the work and will of God in your life. Believe it or not, the most dangerous point of your Christian walk is when you begin to believe that Satan isn't going to bother you any longer. When you quit fighting, he doesn't; and the enemy always tries to be the "aggressor." His tried-and-tested methods of attack are continuous, so you cannot lay down in a firefight and do nothing; the enemy is relentless and will not quit because you have. You must be prepared to fight all the way to the end. You must be ready to make an assault to take the objective.

Go on the offensive today; but remember; a spiritual war is conducted in the same manner as physical warfare: It is directed against the enemy, not against the objective. Satan is the enemy, and we fight him to extract from him what he possesses. *"But no one can enter the strong man's house and take his **property** unless he first binds the strong man"* (Mark 3:27). Now, what on earth is the strong man's property? It is the souls of men and women that Satan holds prisoner through the fear of death. They are subject to his bondage (Hebrews 2:14–15). For this reason, go on the offensive today.

Day 9

Jesus is Victor

The night is almost gone, and the day is at hand.
Romans 13:12a

Just when everything is looking like it could not be worse, God steps in. In the middle of your worst firefight, Jesus will come marching through the fire, and you wonder why you ever were afraid.

Be encouraged. There can be no day without a night, nor a victory without a fight. If there is *bad*, *good* is just around the corner. Victory is for those who put their trust in Jesus and march with Him to the end.

Day 10

Dream Sheet

For our citizenship is in heaven, from which
we eagerly wait for a Savior, the Lord Jesus Christ;
who will transform the body of our humble state
into conformity with the body of His glory.

Philippians 3:20–21

Every soldier looks forward to the day he can fill out his dream sheet. For the entire combat tour, he has thought about other places he'd rather be—Home, on leave, R&R or his next duty station. Dreams of lying in a hammock with white beaches and palm trees swaying in the breeze filled his head.

Writing up a dream sheet is a satisfying affair in the life of a soldier. It's almost as good as the real thing—and most of the time, more thrilling. You see, a battle-worn G.I. doesn't have much in his own grasp, and he doesn't control much more than what his uniform looks like and who his friends are. But when it comes to filling out a dream sheet, he's on his own to do as he likes—at least, on paper!

A dream sheet is like a "wish list" in civilian language. The soldier is called up by the personnel department and asked to indicate what duty assignment he would like to have next. Well, the old saying goes: You don't get anything unless you ask for it. The same is true in the life of a soldier, and the dream sheet makes it all possible. He takes great care in writing his requests down; he wants to make sure that nobody misunderstands a thing.

When the final bugle blows for us here and we are notified that it is time to transfer, we need to make sure that our dream sheets are correctly filled out. We sure wouldn't want to end up in some dreaded duty assignment like hell, would we? Eternity is an awful long time to spend in a place like that.

Let me be your travel agent today. Let me remind you to fill out your dream sheet with the right destination in mind. Jesus said, *"That unless a man be born again, he will not see the kingdom of heaven"* (John 3:3). These are your final instructions, your orders are being cut, but your final destination cannot be determined unless you take the initiative to fill out your dream sheet. You must be born again; you cannot get the good assignment any other way.

Day 11

The Suffering of Soldiers

*But to the degree that you share the sufferings
of Christ, keep rejoicing; so that also at the
revelation of His glory, you may rejoice with exultation.*
1 Peter 4:13

Winemakers around the world know the deeper
a grapevine has to burrow to find water, the better
the grapes will be for the making of wine. In fact, amongst
vintners in France there is a time-honored wisdom called,
la vigne doit souffrir, which means, "the vine must suffer."
They say the more a vine thirsts in an arid vineyard full of
rocks, the deeper its roots must dig through the ground to
find moisture. This gives strength to the branches and
causes them to produce the rich grapes from which the
superb French wines are made.

General Douglas MacArthur once said, "The soldier,
above all others, is required to perform the highest act of

religious teaching—sacrifice." Soldiers, like a suffering grapevine searching for water, put one foot in front of the other and endure a rigorous life. The military life builds character because it stretches people beyond the norm.

As branches of Jesus, the Vine, we Christian soldiers find our strength through pain and suffering. When we have to burrow deep between the stones of this world in search of the living water of Christ, we become a more fruitful vessel in our walk with Him. Personal suffering is the single most effective key to exploring God's ways and truth than any personal good fortune that may come our way.

Suffering is essential for spiritual growth. Suffering is the channel through which human beings are introduced to the spiritual dimensions of their lives. Without suffering, I'm afraid our lives would be so shallow that our lights would be dim and our salt tasteless. The quality of our character is developed while enduring pain—not before and not afterward.

"After suffering for a little while, the God of all grace, who called you to His eternal glory in Christ, will Himself perfect, confirm, strengthen and establish you" (1 Peter 5:10).

Day 12

Doors

The steps of a man are established by the Lord.
Psalm 37:23a

Doors are ways in which God communicates His direction for our lives. While on the daily march, the Lord opens up "doors" of opportunity for us—that's His job. Our duty is to walk through the door and carry out what He will have us do.

This idea of doors has been known to Christians for a long time, and it seems pretty cut and dried; but let me present one more option that you may not have considered. What if God opens a door that He never intended you to walk through in the first place? Do you still walk through it just because God opened it?

You may ask, "Why would He do that?" Good question. Why would God open a door of opportunity and not want us to walk through it? Does God set us up to be tempted or ambushed? Of course not. God does not tempt, but He does *test* His servants. Sometimes doors are opened by Him to see how well we are doing with our life lessons. Are we dying to self, striving to be God-centered and holy, and are we willing to let Him be enough in our lives—or do we still think we need more?

God is in the business of purifying His servants. He wants to bring us unto Him. Our lives are really a series of doors opening and closing, all by His will, to draw us near. Be on the alert! There are valuable lessons at the threshold of each one. Be sensitive to identify Him and His ways. And be quick to answer when He knocks.

Day 13

Don't Forget Your Buddy

A friend loves at all times.
Proverbs 17:17

We are NOT primarily put on this earth to see through one another, but to see one another through. When a friend goes down, don't leave him wounded in the trail. If he is weak, carry him through for as long as it takes.

God has enlisted you not to judge, but to serve. Serve as long as it takes to complete the mission. As we pass through this combat zone, let us not forget the wounded. We must get as many out of the kill zone before we pass on—it's our duty. In good times and bad, and especially when the going gets rough, don't forget your buddy! Who knows, he may someday have to drag you off the trail to clean up your wounds.

Day 14

Line of March

This is the way...walk in it.
Isaiah 30:21

Just when you think you are lost, along comes your wonderful Pathfinder. He'll be alongside the trail to direct you to every correct fork in the road. Don't step out on your own. Never trust your feelings, only what you know to be true from experience.

Be patient and wait upon the Lord; He is with you always. You can count on this and it is the only certainty you have. Why? Because He loves you with an everlasting love.

Day 15

Patriotism

*And even if He does, let it be
known to you, O king, that we are
not going to serve your gods.*
Daniel 3:18

Patriotism is no more than a high form of commitment. As soldiers, we stand and fight for causes and take our orders from the high command. If we are ordered to walk through fire or give up our lives—or "other" commitments—we walk through the fire simply because we know that our heavenly Commander is ALWAYS with us. If He decides not to deliver us from the earthly fire, we need to take our stand and decide to not take the easy way out. Together we stand. God has a reason for everything in our lives...everything.

Day 16

Tattoos

*Behold I have inscribed you
on the palms of My hands.*
Isaiah 49:16

As a young paratrooper in the army, one of the first things I did after earning my jump wings was go down town and get myself a tattoo. It was the thing to do, not the most brilliant, but neither was jumping from a perfectly good airplane while in flight.

Those days are long gone for me, but every time I bare my upper left arm, I see that ugly fading picture of a parachute; and I am reminded of a time of honor and service in the elite forces of our country.

I was always told by more experienced men that I should never get a tattoo because I would live to regret it. Well, maybe I shouldn't have gotten the doggone thing, but as of yet I haven't lost any sleep over it.

Reading the Bible today caused me to think about tattoos again, but this time it wasn't like before. I thought of something that may encourage you today.

God so loved all of us that He had Jesus, His only Son, die by being nailed to a cross so that we may be saved. The soldiers fastened Him to it with nails driven into His hands and feet. Do you know that when Jesus was resurrected out of the grave to live again, He still had those nail scars? He was "tattooed!" However, His tattoos served a much better purpose than ours—they served to remind Him of us. It says in Isaiah 49:16–17, *"Even these may forget, but I will not forget you. Behold, I have inscribed you on the palms of My hands."* Imagine that! Every time God looks at those indelible scars, He doesn't see dishonor, shame, pain or embarrassment; He only sees us, His children, eternally tattooed where He keeps us—right in the palm of His hands.

Day 17

Following Orders

And the Lord utters His voice before His army.
Joel 2:11

The main duty of a soldier is to obey his commander's orders. Some orders we may not like or agree with and some commanders don't always give the right ones, but our duty is to obey.

If God is the Supreme Commander, and we are troops following His orders, there is nothing to fear. Unlike earthly commanders, His orders are always right, He enters every march and every battle out in front of us. All we have to do is get in step right behind Him and *obey*. Obedience is better than sacrifice any day!

Day 18

The Same God

I the Lord do not change.
Malachi 3:6

God doesn't change—we do. Some days we are flying high with eagles, and we can surely see God up there. Where the real test lies is whether we can see Him on the dull, dreary days of trudging through the foggy valleys of the ordinary routines. Can we see him working even in the mundane duties of our everyday life?

He is there—look a little harder.

Today, remember, He is the same God up on the mountain as the one down in the valley. There is no difference. He is always with you.

Day 19

The Mission

*Truly, truly, I say to you, unless
a grain of wheat falls into the earth
and dies, it remains by itself
alone; but if it dies, it bears fruit.*
John 12:24

Robert E. Lee once said, "A good commander loves his soldiers, but he is also willing to let the thing he loves die in order to accomplish the mission."

Jesus, the only begotten Son of God, was also loved by His commander. He was allowed to die to defeat the enemy in the final battle at the cross of Calvary. God, in His infinite wisdom, knew all along that Jesus would have to go up on that hill, lay himself down on a couple of planks, and let a soldier drive nails in His hands and feet. He knew His son would have to die there in order for victory to be accomplished. The good news is that He paid it so we wouldn't have to. You see, it was our crimes He was dying for—past, present and future. It was sort of like someone going down to your bank and paying off the debt you have on your car or house. You are free from it—it was paid off!

So, what is asked of you? Not much, just believe that Jesus died for you and admit that He is the Son of God (Romans 10:9).

It has become a rescue mission, and the line is hanging down from the chopper. All you gotta do is grab it and hang on for the ride!

Day 20

Sacrifice

Present your bodies a living and
holy sacrifice, acceptable to God,
which is your spiritual service of worship.
Romans 12:1

Sacrifice begins in the unseen places of the heart; places that no one can see except God Himself. However, the deepest sacrifices are not often in the things most obvious to the human eye. They are done in the human heart.

When an animal was sacrificed as an offering, it was offered for another life. When we volunteer ourselves to be sacrificed, we offer ourselves willingly—we have a choice to do it or not.

Sacrifice is one of the measures God continually uses in evaluating our lives. Measure your life by sacrifice. Can we put down the morning paper and read the Bible instead? Can we give up casual conversation and choose prayer instead?

There is another sacrifice that is important: It is giving up the sin of criticism. We must beware of how we measure the sacrifice of others. We must measure our own sacrifices, but let God measure those of other people.

Day 21

Reform the Lines and Attack!

By your endurance you will gain your lives.
Luke 21:19

At the battle of Shiloh, during the Civil War, the first day of fighting gave a dim hope for the Union forces. At the end of the day, a situation report came to General Ulysses S. Grant. He had lost half of his artillery, one third of his infantry and they had been pushed all the way back to the river.

His junior officers asked him, "Sir, what are you going to do?"

Without batting an eye, Grant replied, "What else? Reform the lines and attack!"

The next morning, the Union troops did reform and attack. The Confederates were so caught by surprise that the battle was won in a matter of hours.

When you feel that your walls and lines have been

breached and the enemy is ready to swarm through, re-form your lines and attack! Go to God...read His Word...put on your armor, then step out and look the enemy right in the eye with the intent to bring glory to God...and then attack!

What weapons do we use in this war? The primary weapon is the name of Jesus Christ, *"...That whatever you ask of the Father in my name, He may give to you"* (John 15:16. Bind the enemy—in the name of the Lord! Cut off his influences—in the name of the Lord! And remember, you cannot do this in your name or any other name, but only in the name of Jesus Christ, our Lord and Savior!

Day 22

Volunteers and Draftees

*Joseph, son of David, do not be
afraid to take Mary as your wife.*
Matthew 1:20

When you went into the military were you drafted
or did you volunteer? For most of us, being made to
do something seriously effects our attitude about what
we are "forced" to do. On the other hand, a volunteer has
a choice and that usually makes all the difference in the
world in how our service or duty goes.

Have you ever thought about how Joseph felt when he
discovered that Mary was pregnant...and he hadn't slept
with her?! At first, he wanted to secretly handle the situation, *"And Joseph her husband, being a righteous man,
and not wanting to disgrace her, desired to put her away
secretly"* (Matthew 1:19). But an angel came to him and

44

encouraged him to step up and be brave. Joseph answered the call and did step up. He became a volunteer—he volunteered to be Jesus' dad. He could have easily gotten out of it because, unlike a biological father, he had a choice to be a father or not.

When we make a decision to follow and serve Jesus, we are not draftees—we are volunteers! The *decision* is what makes the difference. God isn't looking for soldiers who have to be drafted. He is looking for those who will step up, be brave and volunteer.

Each day is like that, too. We have the choice to walk with Jesus or walk away from Him. That decision— that *volunteering*— is our primary duty to begin each day with, especially since God isn't into drafting His army.

Day 23

Light on the Path

...For we walk by faith, not by sight
2 Corinthians 5:7

None of us know exactly what the day has in store for us. We can only hope for the best to come out of it.

Like the lone soldier walking out in front of his buddies, he is the point man who looks for enemy signs up ahead. As he walks along, his job is to detect the dangers of ambushes and booby traps that are set up to wound or destroy those who follow and depend on him for their safety.

Our Lord Jesus walks before those who are obedient to follow Him through this life. He is faithful to light up our path. We will be secure in our march today if we stay behind and follow Him. Our problems begin when we lag behind, stray from the unit or get out in front of Jesus— who is our Point Man for life.

Day 24

Let the Past Be the Past at Last

*Forgetting those things which are behind
and reaching forward to those things which are shared.*
Philippians 3:13

How many times do we carry old wounds and memories around like trophies and medals won in some past battle. As painful as some of these experiences are, if we aren't careful they may become permanent fixtures. When we become absorbed with the traumas of our past and begin to depend upon them for our identification and survival, our lives become unreal. They give us a false sense of security...when, in actual fact, they serve to drag us down.

Worry, stress, bitterness and anxiety stemming from a past experience can be objects of turmoil that we strive to overcome, or excuses that keep us from the healing of God.

It is our choice to move ahead in life today. We can choose and claim the recovery of Christ or we can be subject to our own self-inflicted misery by hanging on to the past.

Live today for the Lord, leave yesterday where it was, and let tomorrow be on its own.

Day 25

Surrendering

Submit therefore to God. Resist the devil
and he will flee from you.

James 4:7

A soldier in the world's army is trained to never surrender. The code of conduct for the U.S. military is: "I will never surrender of my own free will...." This code is drilled over and over until it is memorized by all personnel serving in the armed forces. It does, however, work just the opposite in God's army.

To be at peace in our lives and at ease with God, we must first and foremost surrender our lives to Him before we can reap the benefits of being His soldier. We have to *give up* before we can secure the victory for our lives. It is the only requirement for eternal enlistment.

Day 26

Fear

No weapon formed against you will prevail.
Isaiah 54:17

The angel of the Lord encamps around those who fear Him, and He delivers them.

The expressions "fear of God" or "fear God" don't mean that God expects us to cringe in terror every time we hear His name or think of Him. It means we respect and trust Him as our Commander-in-Chief who will never forsake us in times of trouble. The fear of God is the one fear which removes all other fears!

Day 27

Hardship

Endure hardship with us like
a good soldier for Christ Jesus.
2 Timothy 2:3

God allows us to suffer many hardships, and He has a purpose in letting us endure the burdens of this world. It is the root that travels the furthest to reach water that produces the best grapevines. It is from those grapes that the best wine is made.

What coarse finger today is God going to use to squeeze us with? What man or woman will He place upon our path to test and try us? What circumstance will He orchestrate to help hone our faith? It is good to remember that He IS in every detail of our lives—the good, the bad and the ugly.

When our objective seems impossible to reach and there seems to be no possible way to hold up under the circumstances, He will be there. His faith endures for ever.

Day 28

Wounds

...For by His wounds you were healed.
1 Peter 2:24

O nce you have been to war, you know about battllefield wounds. Immediate care for these injuries is critical. Wounds left alone and unclean will become infected and lead to further complications. If you were tending to a casualty, you would never think of putting a battle-dress bandage over the dirty flesh wound without first applying antiseptic. You would first clean it out, and then wrap it.

Wounds of the heart and spirit are treated like this as well. You can't just cover them up and think they will go away. If you have been hurt or wronged unjustly, if you have bitterness or unforgiveness, the only lasting "antiseptic" is the oil of Jesus Christ, *"By His stripes you are healed"*.

Give all your hurts to Jesus today—let Him do the comforting and cleaning.

Day 29

Survival Skills

*And these words which I command you
today shall be in your heart.*
Deuteronomy 6:6

To survive in this world, we must have God's word firmly placed in our hearts. Begin each day by reading, studying and meditating upon what God is saying in the Holy Scriptures. Let the Bible be your "soldiers manual"; hide the words away inside, and obey them. Someday you may not have a Bible handy, and you will have to rely upon your skill to remember the words which have been imprinted in your heart and mind— that's survival!

Day 30

God Loves Failures

*Assuredly, I say to you that it is hard for a
rich man to enter the kingdom of heaven.*
Matthew 19:23

Few men ever come to a saving grace through Jesus
Christ in good times. Unfortunately, it usually takes
a disaster or a crisis and almost always embraces a threat
of failure.

Why is it hard for a rich man to enter heaven? It is
because a man who needs no help here on earth finds it
too difficult or unnecessary to seek after God with his
whole heart.

You, the poor in spirit, will inherit the kingdom of God—
you are called blessed. The Lord is our friend in good
times and He is our deliverer in the bad. He welcomes
our failures because He knows that when we fail on our
own power, there's a good chance we will turn to Him for
His.

If you don't have enough power, you aren't weak enough!

Day 31

Choosing Sides

He who is not with me is against me.
Matthew 12:30

When our friends give us an ultimatum to choose between them or our faith, what will it be for you? It may be easy to say, "I'll take God any day!" But will it really be that easy? When the chips are down and all you can see are your friends and what they have, I encourage you to choose God. He will restore those things that you fear losing...if it is in His will. Pray for His will to be done today.

What good does it do any of us to take the side of man over God? On the other hand, what good would it do me to choose God over man? It would mean everything— eternally! I choose God.

Day 32

Laying Tracks

*Therefore I say to you, all things
for which you pray and ask,
believe that you have received them,
and they shall be granted to you.*
Mark 11:24

Why pray? Why do we, His mere created ones, need to ask God to do anything? Surely, He can do whatever He wants without the aid of our requests...after all, He is God! This is a great mystery, but it is also the truth.

Likewise, isn't it a bit odd that the "created" would have to *knock* before the "Creator" would open the door? It is also more than peculiar that the "clay" has to *ask* before it can *receive* from the "Potter." Won't the Potter (God) just give the clay (us) things without our asking? It is almost mind-boggling that we, mere mortals, are commanded to pray before our Creator will take action. But why is this?

Like every good tactician, God likes teamwork. He desires to work with us to make changes, and He gave us the gift of free will in order to join Him in these endeavors. Part of the equipment in this thing called willpower is our prayer-power.

Our prayers are so important to make changes that God waits for them before He moves. Let us picture God as a huge, all-powerful locomotive sitting on unfinished railroad tracks. His engines are on and He is ready to roll, but He will not budge until we join Him in the operation. Our prayers are like those tracks laid out before Him to run on. Oh sure, God can do anything without us—He, too, has free will. However, He chooses to wait for our appeal before taking action. Pray...ask...receive.

Day 33

The Elite Soldier

*Then God said, 'Let Us
make man in Our image,
according to Our likeness....'*
Genesis 1:26a

First there was God. God is a Spirit. Second, He
created angels. Angels are spirit. Then, He created
the material universe—the earth, heavens, elements and
the animals— and then He made man, both spirit and material. What a wonderful distinction we have!

God not only created us in His image, but He made us
in the image of the physical universe as well. Not even
God or the angels have that uniqueness. At any given time,
we can choose to be either in the spirit realm or the physical realm. When we pray and worship God we enter into
the spirit realm, and when we do not fellowship with Him
we are in the material realm.

We are elite soldiers, capable of doing mighty things. We can think, drive cars, run computers, anticipate future things and make choices. We have incredible power on our own, but have the most power when we are weak and have to enter the spirit realm to rely completely on God to see us through. We must decrease and allow Him to increase to be victorious.

Day 34

Rearguard

...And the glory of the Lord
will be your rearguard.
Isaiah 58:8

There's no need to watch your backside any longer. You don't have put your back against the wall in public places. Why watch your backtrail? The Lord not only equips you with the full armor (Ephesians 6:10–18) to protect yourself from the front, but He also provides security for your rear as well. He is your Rock, your Fortress and your Deliverer. Put your trust in Him and rest in His arms today.

Day 35

Reveille

*Awake, sleeper, and arise from your sleep,
and Christ will shine on you.*
Ephesians 5:14

Answer that bugle call today. Get up and come alive by seeking the Lord Jesus at first light. Surrender to Him as soon as your eyes open and ask Him to take you captive for the day. When you hear the call, don't delay. You don't want to miss the things God has in store for you. Already the hour for you to awake has come. Christ's salvation is nearer to you than ever before. Ask and you will receive.

Day 36

The Night is Over

The night is almost gone, and the day is at hand.
Let us lay aside the deeds of darkness and
put on the armor of light.
Romans 13:12

It is our choice to lay aside improper behavior. We can either answer the call of God's Spirit, each day, or the call of the flesh. One will give you life and the other death. It is your choice and if you can't make up your mind, let God do it for you. Give your weaknesses to Him because He wants to carry your burdens for you. He won't take them unless you give them. Submit to God and watch your enemies flee!

Day 37

Follow Me

My sheep hear My voice, and I
know them, and they follow Me.
John 10:27

Leaders are meant to be followed, but it takes a degree of discipline to do that. When Jesus told His disciples to follow Him, He was asking them to discipline themselves for the march. He wanted them to walk as He walked and where He walked. He expected them to become the same leader that He was—without practicing sin or offending others. Practice discipline today in all areas of your life and see how much more you get done...with little or no stress. Live to follow and serve, and you will likely end up leading as Jesus did. Be a role model as He was to you.

Day 38

Taking Prisoners

*...We are taking every thought captive
to the obedience of Christ.*
2 Corinthians 10:5

Satan may tempt and try you, but your own thoughts can be your primary enemy. If you allow them to roam freely with no control, you will never win the war. Much like an army that loses a war because it would only fight on warm, sunny days, you cannot afford to be slack when the storms come. You must determine to take every thought captive in both the good times and the bad. The days of sunshine soldiers and fair-weather patriots are over—prepare your self in thought and action.

Day 39

A Soldier's Confession

*And when the centurion, who was
standing right in front of Him, saw
the way He breathed His last, he said,
"Truly this man was the Son of God."*
Mark 15:39

It is by no coincidence that one of the first non-Jews
to recognize and confess Jesus as the Messiah, was a
soldier at the foot of the cross. Undoubtedly, he was one
of the first to be sprinkled with the blood of our Savior.
God has a special place in His heart for soldiers. He has
planned it so that every Christian fits into this model. We
are all to be called a soldier in His army—men and women
under authority, obedient even to death.

Day 40

The Long March

And they each march in line,
nor do they deviate from their paths.
Joel 2:7

At the end of each long march, there is not a more welcome sight than our own base camp. The sight of it off in the distance strengthens and encourages us. No matter what the pain has been on the long march, it has been worth it all. Regardless of the sufferings along the way and the price we have had to pay, it all pales in comparison to the rewards of coming home.

Base camp is home— it has hot showers and food, and is a place to apply the ointment to our sore feet. Keep your eyes upon the heavenly home; don't get off the path. It will be worth every ounce of sweat that has been left along the trail.

For additional copies of ***Point Man in Your Pocket***
Send $2.99 + $1.50 shipping and handling to:

P.O. Box 68065
Seattle, WA 98168

Email:chuckdean@namvetbook.com

For veteran-related issues and ministry opportunities, contact:

Point Man International Ministries

Hotline:
(800) 877–VETS
Home Page:
http://www.mcpages.com/PointMan/